W9-BNL-907

A Chocolate Moose
for Dinner

written and illustrated by
FRED GWYNNE

Aladdin Paperbacks

Aladdin Paperbacks
An imprint of Simon & Schuster
Children's Publishing Division
1230 Avenue of the Americas
New York, NY 10020
Copyright © 1976 by Fred Gwynne
All rights reserved including the right of reproduction
in whole or in part in any form.
Originally published by Windmill Books, Inc. and Wanderer Books

Designed by Dorothea von Elbe
Manufactured in the United States of America

30 29 28 27 26 25 24 23

Library of Congress Cataloging in Publication Data
Gwynne, Fred.
   A chocolate moose for dinner.
   SUMMARY: A little girl pictures the things her
parents talk about, such as a chocolate moose,
a gorilla war, and shoe trees.
   1. English language—Homonyms—Juvenile
literature.   [1. English language—Homonyms.
2. English language—Terms and phrases]   I. Title
PE1595.G73   1980   428.1   80-14150
ISBN 0-671-66741-6

For Keiron, Gaynor, Madyn, Evan, and Furlaud

Mommy says she had a chocolate moose for dinner last night.

And after dinner

she toasted Daddy.

there's a gorilla war.

Daddy says
he has trees
for all his shoes.

**Daddy says
lions pray on**

other  animals.

Daddy says he hates

the arms race.

Daddy says there should

Mommy says her

favorite painter is Dolly.

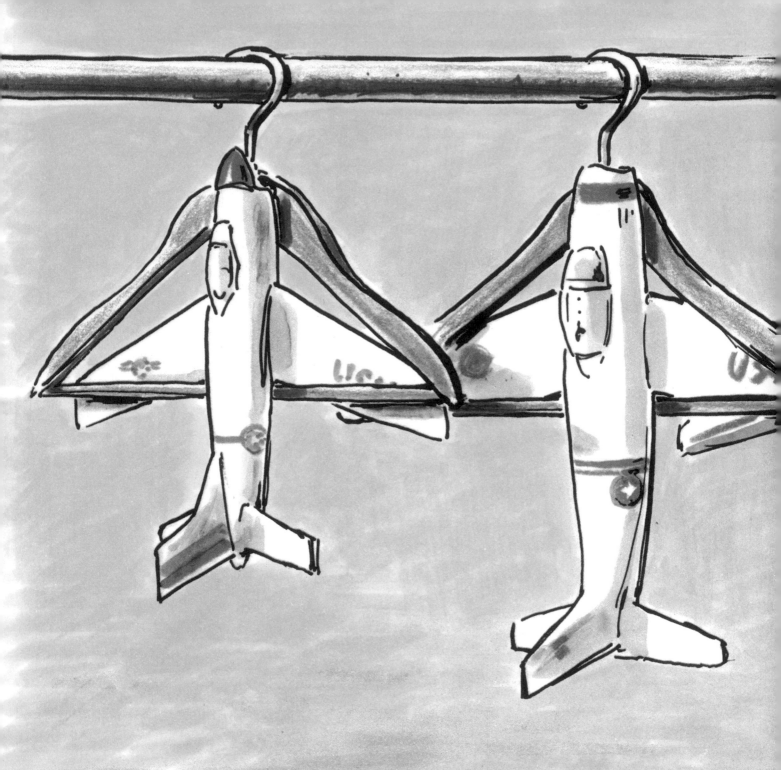

**Mommy says
there are airplane hangers.**

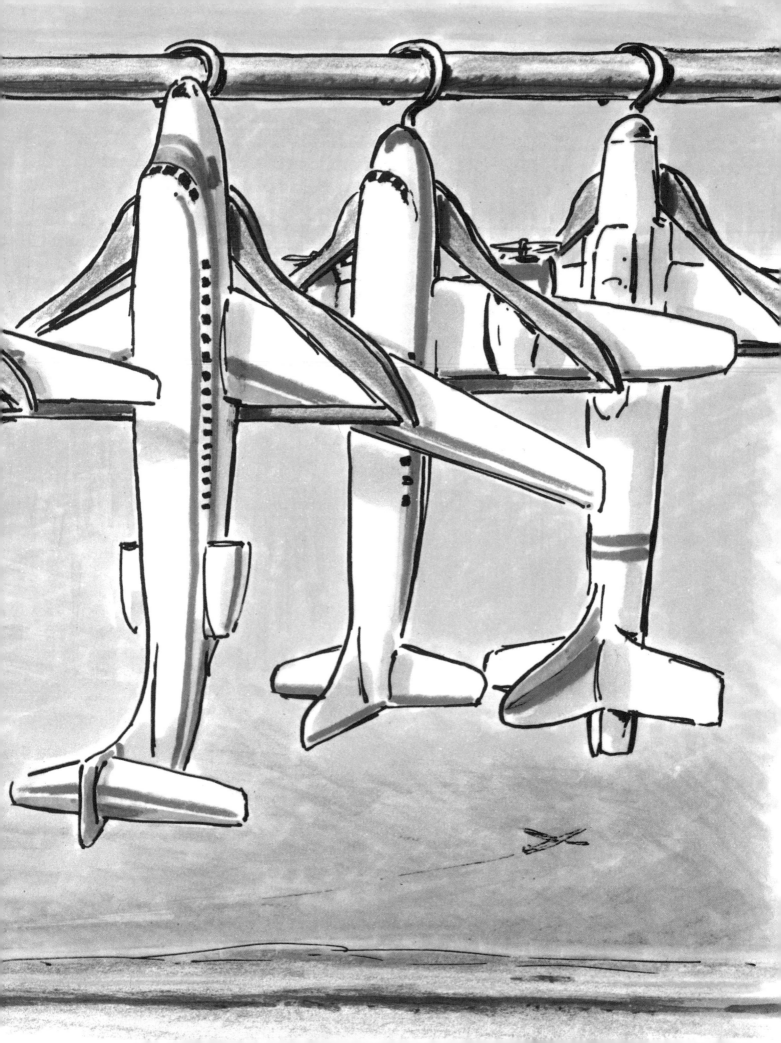

Daddy says he has the best fishing tackle.

**It says on TV
a man held up a bank.**

He spent two years in the pen.

And he has just escaped and is now on the lamb.

At the ocean Daddy says

watch out for the under toe.

Daddy says he plays
the piano by ear.

Daddy says that in college

people row in shells.

**And some row
in a single skull.**

Mommy says she's going to tell me about Santa Claws.

And Daddy says he's going to tell me the story of

the tortoise and the hair.

**Stories
like these
drive me
up a wall!**